Understanding the Cultures of the Middle East

Religion, Philosophy, and Nationalism across the Middle East

Katie Griffiths

Cavendish Square
New York

Published in 2017 by Cavendish Square Publishing, LLC
243 5th Avenue, Suite 136, New York, NY 10016

First Edition

CPSIA Compliance Information: Batch #CW17CSQ

All websites were available and accurate when this book was sent to press.

Library of Congress Cataloging-in-Publication Data

Names: Griffiths, Katie.
Title: Religion, philosophy, and nationalism across the Middle East / Katie Griffiths.
Description: New York : Cavendish Square, 2017. | Series: Understanding
the cultures of the Middle East | Includes index.
Identifiers: ISBN 9781502623591 (library bound) | ISBN 9781502623607 (ebook)
Subjects: LCSH: Middle East--Juvenile literature. | Middle East--Religion-
-Juvenile literature. | Middle East--History--Juvenile literature.
Classification: LCC DS44.G75 2017 | DDC 956--dc23

Editorial Director: David McNamara
Editor: Elizabeth Schmermund
Copy Editor: Rebecca Rohan
Associate Art Director: Amy Greenan
Designer: Alan Sliwinski
Production Coordinator: Karol Szymczuk
Photo Research: J8 Media

The photographs in this book are used by permission and through the courtesy of: Cover Jose Fuste Raga/Getty Images; p. 4 Aysegul Muhcu/Alamy Stock Photo; p. 10 Prmustafa/iStock/Thinkstock.com; p. 12 Fine Art Images/Heritage Images/Getty Images; p. 17 Paul Prescott/Shutterstock.com; p. 21 ChameleonsEye/Shutterstock.com; p. 26 Predrag Vuckovic/iStockphoto.com; p. 31 Bettmann/Getty Images; p. 35 PATRICK BAZ/AFP/Getty Images; p. 40 Paul Cowan/Shutterstock.com; p. 42 Sher's Photography/Getty Images; p. 45 Romrodphoto/Shutterstock.com; p. 46 Mohannad Khatib/Shutterstock.com; p. 48 Ibrahim Ramadan/Anadolu Agency/Getty Images; p. 53 Mikhail Markovskiy/Shutterstock.com; p. 56 Adwo/Shutterstock.com; p. 58 Robert Landau/Getty Images; p. 62 Popperfoto/Getty Images; p. 66 Gavin Hellier/Getty Images; p. 70 Photo12/UIG via Getty Images; p. 73 Alinari/Alinari via Getty Images; p. 77 Zaid echair/File:Mosque hassan ll – CASABLANCA.jpg/Wikimedia Commons; p. 79 Yassine Gaidi/Anadolu Agency/Getty Images; p. 82 AFP/Getty Images; p. 85 Sueddeutsche Zeitung Photo/Alamy Stock Photo; p. 88 TOUSSAINT KLUITERS/AFP/Getty Images; p. 93 Bettmann/Getty Images; p. 97 Thierry Chesnot/Getty Images; p. 99 REPORTERS ASSOCIES/Gamma-Rapho via Getty Images.

Printed in the United States of America

Contents

This map shows the Ottoman Empire, many parts of which now form the modern Middle East.

Introduction

The Middle East is a complex and often misunderstood region. It has been stereotyped in both positive and negative ways, defined by Western perceptions and reduced to stock images of oil reserves, the repression of women, and terrorist activity. However, this region is far more interesting and nuanced than has been usually shown in Western media. It is an area with a vast variety of cultures and ideologies.

The Middle East is usually defined as a transcontinental area covering western Asia, southeastern Europe, and northern Africa. The region can be referred to both as the

"Middle East" and the "Near East," and both of these terms can be highly problematic. The term "Middle East" was first popularized by American naval strategist Alfred Thayer Mahan in 1902 and was meant to signify the area between the Arabian Peninsula and India. Mahan was already very conscious of how politically important the region, and in particular its center in the Persian Gulf, was likely to become over the following century. However, modern critics have argued that using the names "Middle East" and "Near East" show a **Eurocentric** attitude that defines regions outside of Europe as somehow less important on the world stage.

The region contains many different ethnic groups, yet the majority of its peoples are Arabs, Azeris, Kurds, Persians, and Turks. As well as its variety of people, it is also the birthplace of some of the world's most prominent religions, including Christianity, Judaism, and Islam. In fact, some of humankind's earliest and most advanced civilizations were born here; Mesopotamia, comprising modern-day Iraq, Syria, and Kuwait, was one of the world's "cradles of civilization."

Due to its large scale, the Middle East is often divided into three subregions to discuss the countries it contains. These are the Gulf region, the Levant region, and North Africa. The Gulf region is home to Oman, United Arab Emirates, Saudi Arabia, Yemen, Qatar, Bahrain, Kuwait, Iraq, and Iran. The Levant region consists of Egypt, Jordan, Lebanon, Israel, Palestine, and Syria. Finally, the North Africa section of the Middle East comprises Libya, Algeria, Morocco, and Tunisia.

The Middle East was created out of the remains of what was known as the Ottoman Empire. Founded in 1299 by Oguz Turks, the empire began under the rule of Osman I in northwestern Anatolia (now modern-day Turkey). At the height of its power, it was the center for East-West interactions for six centuries, but after repeated military defeats and setbacks against Western powers in the late nineteenth century, the empire's size and power began to decline. Prior to World War I, the Ottoman Empire comprised roughly thirty-eight modern-day countries, though these numbers did fluctuate during the Ottoman reign. It even occupied parts of Iran, Russia, Italy, Austria, Czech Republic, Slovakia, Poland, Djibouti, Somalia and Malta.

In 1914, Ottoman leader Enver Pasha joined the First World War on the side of Germany against Britain and France in effort to win back lost territories. Britain immediately perceived the Ottoman Empire as the "weak link," believing that if the Ottomans could be defeated then the rest of the alliance would fall. British powers began to encourage revolution in Ottoman territory in order to undermine their power. Political uprisings combined with military force would later prove to be the undoing of the Ottoman Empire, as it was defeated first by an Arab uprising in 1916, and then later by British forces in 1918.

What happened next would be seen by Middle Eastern nations as an Anglo-French betrayal for generations to come. In a secret treaty, known as the Sykes-Picot Agreement, the British and French governments divided up the territories of the Middle East between themselves into so-called "spheres of influence."

This occurred despite the fact that British emissaries had promised to establish an autonomous Arab homeland in exchange for military support during the war. France took Syria and Lebanon, turning them into **protectorates**. Britain laid claim to Iraq and Palestine and placed them both under British **mandate**. When the Ottomans had first departed, Arabs had attempted to proclaim an independent state in Damascus; however, it was soon apparent that they lacked the military and economic resources to resist European powers for long.

Britain declared Iraq to be a kingdom, placing the son of ally Sharif Hussein on the throne, and split Palestine in half. Eastern Palestine became the "Emirate of Transjordan," while western Palestine was placed under direct British administration. The British government had promised the international Zionist movement their support in recreating the historical Jewish homeland in Palestine during a time of increased anti-Semitism, particularly in Eastern Europe. This promise led to the introduction of far-reaching privileges for Jewish Palestinians, while revolts from Arab Palestinians were suppressed. As the century progressed into the 1930s, most of the Arabian Peninsula fell under the control of another British ally, Ibn Saud, who refashioned the territory into the kingdom of Saudi Arabia. The map of the region was redrawn, creating countries that included various cultures, ethnicities, and languages in their boundaries, which were normally ruled over by either the Western powers directly or by a ruler allied with them. Most countries within the Middle East remained under some kind of foreign rule until after the Second World War, when they finally became independent or were restored to independence.

The first half of the twentieth century established the contemporary map of the Middle East; however, it also laid the groundwork for many modern-day conflicts and political issues. The Sykes-Picot Agreement was drawn up without a complete knowledge of the region's ethnic and religious divides, thus creating tensions that would reach boiling point over the next few decades. While there are similarities in the philosophical thinking, nationalistic beliefs, and religious practices between various countries, each country has its own blend of cultures and practices, which together make up the rich tapestry of the Middle East.

The Grand Mosque is located in the holy city of Mecca, Saudi Arabia.

1

The History of Religion, Philosophy, and Nationalism across the Middle East

Today's Middle East was not created in a vacuum, but instead was the result of hundreds of years of social movements, political revolutions, and philosophical ideologies. Exploring each of the Middle East's three regions requires a basic understanding of the entire area. This chapter illustrates not just the physical outlines of the region, but also how key elements of the area's religious, philosophical, and national history developed and changed over time.

The Building Blocks of the Middle East

Most often, when discussing the Middle East, the area is broken into three distinct regions: the Gulf region, the Levant region, and North Africa.

The Gulf is the region of the Middle East bordering what the Western world knows as the Persian Gulf, a Mediterranean sea in Western Asia. The Gulf states within the region are Oman, the

Constantinople (now Istanbul) under Ottoman rule

United Arab Emirates, Saudi Arabia, Yemen, Qatar, Bahrain, Kuwait, Iraq, and Iran. Many of these countries also form part of the Cooperation Council for the Arab States of the Gulf (formerly known as the GCC). The only states that are not members are Iraq, Yemen, and Iran. Saudi Arabia and Iran are the two largest countries of the region and are also the two most powerful religious forces in the region with different practices of Islam. Saudi Arabia shares borders with Oman, Yemen, the United Arab Emirates, Qatar, Kuwait and Iraq. Iran shares a border with Iraq. The region is high in oil resources.

The Levant region lies to the northwest of the Gulf and comprises the following states: Egypt, Lebanon, Jordan, Israel, Palestine, and Syria. Levant is a historical geographical term and comes from the Italian word *levante*, meaning "rising." The term is meant to imply the rising of the sun in the east. The term "Levant states" has also been used to refer to the French mandate over Syria and Lebanon after World War I. The area stands at the crossroads of western Asia, the eastern Mediterranean, and northeast Africa. Egypt is the largest of the Levant countries and borders Israel. Syria shares a border with Lebanon, Jordan, and Israel.

North Africa refers to the northernmost area of the continent of Africa and is bordered by the Mediterranean Sea. It is also frequently known as the Maghreb, which means "sunset" in Arabic, alluding to its western location in the region. Though not traditionally associated with the Arab world, Islamic influence is strong in this region and North Africa is a major part of the Islamic world. The largest country within the region is Algeria, which shares land borders with Morocco, Tunisia, and Libya. Sometimes the country of Mauritania is included within the region, although for the purposes of this text it has not been included.

The Political Development of the Middle East

The modern Middle East was arguably shaped by the events of World War I, but another key element of its development began many centuries earlier with the Ottoman Empire. Also known as the Turkish Empire, the Ottoman Empire was founded in 1299 by a Turkish tribal confederation and lasted until the early twentieth century. Its vast territory included much of the Balkans, Anatolia, central Asia to the borders of Iran, and most of North Africa. It was a multiethnic, multireligious empire made up of largely independent states and ruled largely by Islamic law and the **sultan**'s orders. In its time, it was a world power and a significant player in European politics. In fact, it ruled one quarter of Europe until the eighteenth century. However, from the eighteenth century onwards, its political and military power began to seriously wane and increased European **imperialism** gradually captured its territories.

As Ottoman control weakened, the great powers of Europe (Britain, France, Germany, and Russia) fought to control natural resources, create markets for their national industries, and establish colonies across the Middle East. As they competed for global and economic influence in the fading Ottoman Empire, many Ottoman intellectuals attempted to fight back. Intellectuals like

Jamal al-Din al-Afghani called for a reinterpretation of Islamic principles for the modern world as a method of breaking free from European imperialism. **Secular** nationalist movements arose, such as the Young Turks of Anatolia. Such movements were particularly strong in non-Muslim communities, where members could not fully participate in Islamic nationalist movements. Nationalism within individual states began to challenge Ottoman authority and further weaken its power.

During World War I, an already weakened Ottoman Empire crumbled in the face of national uprisings and British forces and was subsequently divided up amongst the French and British. This directly contradicted promises Britain had made to ally states within the Ottoman Empire that Britain would support their right to independence. It was not until after the Second World War, and the end of British, French and Soviet administration in many parts of the Middle East, that individual states had their independence restored or gained their independence for the first time. With the decline of British influence within the region, and the West's increasing reliance on oil, the United States developed a growing presence in the region from the 1950s onwards.

The Middle East once again became embroiled in Western politics during the Cold War, which pitted the Soviet Union's communist regime against Western democratic governments. In the second half of the twentieth century, the Soviet Union began to align itself with anti-Western regimes and Arab socialist leaders, such as Gamal Abdel Nasser of Egypt and Saddam Hussein of Iraq. The region became the setting for an ideological struggle between America, Russia, and their respective allies. Each side attempted to influence their regional allies within the Middle East, often using internal conflicts between countries or within a single country to their advantage.

The effects of this are still felt today in the heavily anti-Western ideology of many Islamist groups and political parties.

The Development of Middle Eastern Religions

Three major religions originated in the Middle East: Judaism, Christianity, and Islam. There are also many smaller religions practiced throughout the region, such as the **Baha'i Faith**, **Druze**, **Yazidism**, and **Zoroastrianism**. However, Islam is the most prevalent.

Judaism is the oldest surviving monotheistic religion in the world. According to Jewish tradition, it was established around 1812 BCE in the eastern Mediterranean and began with a covenant between Abraham and God. A community of Jews traditionally inhabited historic Palestine, however, in the year 73 CE, the Roman Empire dispersed the Jews after an insurrection against Roman authority. Most Jews then lived as minorities within different communities until the founding of the state of Israel in 1948.

Christianity was originally an offshoot of Judaism, beginning in the first century with the teachings of Jesus of Nazareth. Early Christian communities were often persecuted, until the Roman emperor Constantine converted to Christianity in 324 CE. Many early Christian saints lived in the Middle East. This is also where the tradition of asceticism, the denial of physical pleasures in order to get closer to God, was first developed. There are many different Christian sects across the region, such as Copts, Maronites, Russian Orthodox, Greek Orthodox, Assyrians, and Protestants. The Coptic Church is the most dominant form of Christianity in Egypt. The Maronite Church began in the fifth century and was created by the followers of a Syrian priest called Maroun. The head of the Church, the Maronite Patriarch, is based in Lebanon

Jews praying at the Western Wall in Jerusalem, Israel

where he leads Maronite followers. Maronites are still one of the most powerful political groups in Lebanon. Large Christian communities of different sects can also be found in Syria, Jordan, the West Bank, and Iraq.

Islam first arose at the beginning of the seventh century in the desert community of Mecca in modern-day Saudi Arabia with the revelations of the Prophet Muhammad. It developed out of both Judeo-Christian traditions and the cultural values of the nomadic tribes of Arabia. Through conquest and cultural expansion, the religion spread into parts of the Byzantine and Sassanian Empires, which were respectively Christian and Zoroastrian but which both contained diverse populations. By the middle of the eighth century, Islam had traveled into North Africa, Central Asia, and even southern Europe. (Islamic forces were turned back from the northernmost point of Islamic expansion in France during the Battle of Tours in 732 CE.) Over the centuries, Islam gained followers in Sub-Saharan Africa, South Asia, and Southeast Asia. As each new society adopted Islam, they also created their own version of the religion by incorporating their previous cultural traditions. As a result, many different communities developed within Islam, and many of the divisions within modern-day Islam began as political and **doctrinal** differences between communities. There are also many branches of Islam, with the major **denominations** being Sunni and Shia Islam. This division occurred early on in the history of Islam over disagreements of who would lead the Islamic community following the Prophet Muhammad's death. Sunni Muslims make up the large majority of Muslims in the world at approximately 87 percent, while

Shiites make up between 10 and 13 percent. It is important to understand the historical tension in the Middle East between these two denominations in order to understand contemporary political and nationalist movements in the region.

The Development of Middle Eastern Nationalism

Within the Middle East there are two important and overarching strands of nationalist thought: Pan-Arabism and Arab nationalism. In many ways, they are two halves of the same argument: one ideology calling for Arab cooperation and the other using history and culture to legitimize and solidify Arab unity.

Pan-Arabism is an ideology that calls for the unification of North African and West Asian countries from the Atlantic Ocean to the Arabian Sea. Its advocates often argue in terms of socialist principles and strongly oppose Western political involvement in Arab world affairs. Though it is closely related to Arab nationalism, it has its own philosophy and history. The origins of Pan-Arabism can be found in the work of Jurji Zaydan, a Lebanese writer and teacher, and the *Nahda*, or "awakening," which was an Arab cultural renaissance in the late nineteenth and early twentieth century that began in Egypt. Zaydan promoted a modernized version of the Quranic Arabic that was being adopted as the universal written and official language throughout the Arab world, and which was considered more accessible to the common people. This form of Arabic would later become known as Modern Standard Arabic. Pan-Arabism was first used as a legitimate political movement by Sharif Hussein ibn Ali, the Sharif of Mecca, who sought independence for Mashreq Arabs from the Ottoman Empire and the establishment of a unified Arab state in Mashreq, a region located east of Egypt. By the 1930s, Pan-Arabism had been formalized as a political theory and was being advocated by leading Syrian thinkers such as Constantin Zureiq, Zaki al-Arsuzi and Michel Aflaq, key figures of the Arab Ba'ath Party. Later, it was adopted by the Jordanian King Abdullah I as part of his plan to create a "Greater Syria" by uniting Syria, Palestine, and Jordan under his own leadership. Distrust of Abdullah's expansionist dreams was one of the primary reasons for the founding of the Arab League, a regional organization that aims to safeguard Middle Eastern interests, in 1945.

Arab Nationalism is a nationalistic ideology that celebrates Arab culture and history. Its central premise is that the peoples of the Arab world constitute one nation bound together by a common heritage. This is based on the idea that the Arab nation was formed through the establishment of Arabic as the universal language of communication, and the spread of Islam as the region's primary religion and culture. One of its main goals is to end Western influence in the Arab world and to remove any Arab governments that are believed to be dependent on Western power. The movement has a long history beginning in the nineteenth century. Intellectual circles in the Levant and Egypt began advocating the concept of loyalty to the "Fatherland" and attributing the technological and political successes of Western Europe to patriotism. From the 1860s onwards, literature produced in the Levant states under Ottoman control began to accuse the Ottoman Turks of betraying

The flag of the Arab Nationalist movement, also used as the flag of the Arab Revolt against Ottoman rule, is now used by the Palestinians as their national flag.

Islam and the Fatherland to Western powers. Scholars promoted historic Islamic military successes and drew parallels between cultural triumphs of the Arabs and the advent of Islam. They also claimed that Ottoman decline had been caused by their deviation from "true" Islam. By the beginning of the twentieth-century, groups of Muslim Arabs embraced an Arab nationalist identity that would form the basis for twentieth-century Arab nationalism. During this century, the movement was greatly influenced by

US-Iran Relations

Diplomatic dialogue between the United States and Iran has long been a source of political, cultural, and economic tension. During the Cold War, the United States became concerned about increasing Soviet influence in the region and backed a 1951 coup against Iran's elected prime minister Mohammed Mossadeq, who had planned to nationalize the Iranian oil industry. In his place, Mohammed Reza, **Shah** of Iran, rose to power. Iranians viewed the pro-Western leader as **authoritarian** and oppressive. He rigorously imposed Western social reforms and used his secret police—and torture—to silence any opposition. Popular hatred of the Shah also tarred the reputation of his American supporters by association.

Since 1995, the United States has placed a **trade embargo** on Iran. However, in 2015, the US successfully led negotiations for a nuclear deal to dismantle Iran's nuclear weapons capabilities. Iran complied with the terms in 2016, which led to the lifting of US sanctions.

Iran is unique within the Middle East for being the only country with which the United States has no formal diplomatic relations. Communication between the two governments is done primarily through the embassies of other countries. Iran has set up a section within the Pakistani embassy in Washington, DC, and the United States operates a US Citizen Services division within the Swiss embassy in Tehran.

thinkers such as the Islamic modernist and revivalist scholar Muhammed Abduh. He believed that Europe had advanced from adopting the modernist ideals of "true" Islam, and that Muslims had corrupted and abandoned "true" Islam, thus causing their decline. In the waning years of Ottoman rule, Arab nationalists became more prominent, but it was not until the First World War that the movement gained real popular appeal. During World War I, Britain had been a major sponsor of Arab nationalist thought and ideology, believing it could be used as a weapon against the Ottoman Empire. However, during the interwar years and the British Mandate, Arab nationalism became an important anti-imperial movement against European rule.

Yet, Arab nationalism and pan-Arabism also have their own critics within the Middle East. The most common complaint leveled against the movement is the lack of importance given to individual nations or states. Many citizens, understandably, want their governments to focus on promoting the welfare of their own people. One example is Gamal Abdel Nasser of Egypt, one of pan-Arabism's greatest supporters. While he would later be seen as a hero in the Arab world for his pan-Arabist policies, many Egyptians soon became frustrated with what they perceived as his lack of emphasis on Egypt's individual political and cultural importance. Together with Syria, Nasser's Egypt formed the basis of the first pan-Arab nation, called the United Arab Republic (UAR) in 1958; tensions within Egypt over the role of Egyptian nationalism versus pan-Arabism led to the UAR's downfall in 1961.

Other critics have also accused the pan-Arabic movement of inciting prejudice against ethnic minorities within countries. Calls for Arab unity have, by their very nature, created ethnic tensions within individual states with populations that include those who do not identify as Arab. One key example is the Berber people. The Berbers, also known as the Imazighen people, are the descendants of pre-Arab inhabitants of North Africa. They are found mostly in Morocco, Algeria, Tunisia, Libya, Egypt, Mali, Niger, and Mauritania. During the twentieth century, pro-Arabism sentiment led many North African countries to establish Arabic as their official language. One consequence of this was that many Berbers had no opportunity to learn or use their native language at school or university, further restricting the practice and spread of Berber culture. Today, Berbers are still fighting for equal recognition and rights in their various countries, but too often their language and political identity have been marginalized or even erased by Arab-majority governments.

The Development of Middle Eastern Philosophy

Early Islamic philosophy began in the early ninth century and lasted until the late twelfth century in a period known as the Islamic Golden Age. It was named for the outpouring of scientific, economic, and cultural contributions that occurred during this time. This period had a crucial influence on the development of modern philosophy and science, and greatly influenced Renaissance Europe. Philosophers such as Ibn Rushd and Ibn Sina were vital in renewing interest in the work of Aristotle, and the scholar Avicenna would later influence thinkers such as William of

Auvergne and Thomas Aquinas. Islamic Golden Age achievements in the field of philosophy include: the development of a strict science of citation or "backing"; the willingness to both accept and challenge authority within the same process; the recognition that science and philosophy are both subordinate to morality; the separation of theology and law; early ideas of evolution; the distinction between religion and philosophy; and the development of the philosophical novel.

Contemporary Islamic philosophers have gone on to revive some of the trends of early and medieval Islamic philosophy. These include ethics in science and law, and the duty of Muslims and the role of Islam in forming ethical and legal codes, in particular *fiqh*, or "**jurisprudence**," and *jihad*, or "struggling." The Iranian cleric and philosopher Morteza Motahhari was a key figure in developing the philosophy of the Iranian Republic in the 1960s. The work of Iraqi scholar Muhammad Baqir al-Sadr, published in the 1970s, often focused on his view of the modern-day Islamic state, and included showing how religion and scientific knowledge did not need to be incompatible. The modern Moroccan philosopher Taha Abdurrahman has written extensively on his formulation of an Islamic form of modernity. Today, philosophy is most notably debated in the Middle East in the use and reach of *sharia*, or "religious law," the rights and position of women, and the acceptance or refusal to adapt Islam to modern Western ideals.

Abu Dhabi is the capital city of the United Arab Emirates and a key city of the Persian Gulf.

2

Modern-Day Religion, Philosophy, and Nationalism in the Gulf

The Gulf region of the modern Middle East is the territory around the Persian Gulf, a Mediterranean sea in Western Asia. Historically, the area has also been known as the Persian Gulf, although it is sometimes referred to as the Arabian Gulf or, simply, the Gulf. This choice is a political one and the name "Arabian Gulf" is used prominently by Arab governments. In classical Greek writings, it was referred to as the "Red Sea."

The countries surrounding this sea are known as the Gulf states, and it is in this region where the world's largest single source of crude oil can be found. Oil is a major part of the economy for many Gulf states and led to vast wealth after independence was gained from **colonial** occupation.

Like much of the Middle East, the Gulf region is predominantly Islamic, though there are still other religious minorities. The two main practiced denominations of Islam are Sunni and Shia Islam. The ultraconservative branch of Sunni Islam, known as Wahhabism, is also increasingly popular in the region, particularly in Saudi Arabia, where Wahhabism was born. The philosophies of the region are similarly split. Some states seek to reconcile religious Islamic thought with life in modern globalized societies. Others reject modernism as a Western imperialist intrusion, believing a return to the original principles of Islam would create a better state.

Lastly, when exploring national identity within the region, it is important to understand how each country's individual history has affected how its population understands the concept of nationalism. In *Nationalism in the Gulf States*, scholar Neil Patrick argues:

> *[T]he concept of nation in the Gulf Arab countries is underdeveloped to the extent that the emergent public debate about ways to protect national identity has not yet defined what is meant by 'national.'*

What this means is that tribal affiliation (and **tribalism**) in many Gulf Arab countries is more important than national affiliation or nationalism. A member of a particular tribe in Saudi

Arabia, for example, would likely feel closer to his or her fellow tribe members than to Saudi Arabians of other tribal affiliations. Each state approaches this issue differently, however.

Bahrain

A former British protectorate, the Kingdom of Bahrain declared independence in August 1971. Within the same year, it had signed a new treaty of friendship with Britain, joined the United Nations, and enrolled as a member of the Arab League. The state is often characterized by its mix of modern infrastructure and Persian identity. Among Shia citizens, there are two main ethnic groups: Bahraini and Ajam. The Ajam are ethnic non-Arab Persians whose ancestors arrived from Iran in the early twentieth century. They distinctively identify themselves as Persian Bahrainis or Bahrainis rather than Iranians. Persian culture has influenced the country in a number of ways. The Bahraini dialect borrows many words from the Persian language and several staples of Bahrain's local cuisine have been taken or adapted from Persian dishes, such as *mahyawa*, a savory sauce made from sardines and consumed with bread, and *pishoo*, made from rose water and agar.

Like many Middle Eastern countries, Islam is the country's main faith. However, Bahrainis are noted within the region for their particular tolerance of other religions. Unlike the majority of Gulf states, Bahrain has a significant Shiite majority, though the state is ruled by a Sunni monarchy. This disparity in religious allegiance led to a popular uprising in 2011, when the majority Shia population began protesting against its Sunni rulers. Inspired by the **Arab Spring** movement, protestors also demonstrated in favor of greater political freedom and political equality for Shiites. The government initially allowed the protests, but later King Hamad declared martial law and placed the country under a three-month state of emergency. The government eventually set up an independent commission to investigate the causes of the uprising, winning praise from Western governments. However, many of the commission's recommendations were not implemented and, in 2012, observers from the human rights organization Freedom House were denied entry into the country.

Tolerance forms a major part of the Bahraini mindset. Its citizens are known for their ethnic diversity and religious tolerance. Marriages between Bahrainis and expats are not uncommon. The country's Jewish community is active in public life. Bahrain has one of the largest Christian minorities within the Arab states of the Gulf, and there are many Catholic and Orthodox churches.

Iran

The Islamic Republic of Iran was born out of the 1979 Iranian Revolution, converting the ancient kingdom into a republican state.

Iranian nationalism became a major political force during the twentieth century after an almost bloodless constitutional revolution created Iran's first parliament in 1906. This led to the rise of Reza Shah (*Shah* means "king" in Persian) and the Pahlavi dynasty. They sought to infuse Iranian nationalism with secular ideology and to diminish the influence of Islam on Iranian public life. Reza Shah's aim was to modernize Iran and reduce the power

Iranians pull down a statue of Shah Reza Pahlavi during the 1979 revolution.

of the religious **mullahs**. However, his attempts to do so alienated both hardline religious groups and liberal Iranian intellectuals. The Shah's use of secret police and torture sowed the seeds of the 1979 revolution, during which nationalists fought alongside Islamists to bring down Reza Shah. After the revolution, however, Iranian nationalists found themselves alienated from the new Islamist government.

Within Iran's religious sphere, the majority of its population is Shiite, practicing a branch of Shia known as "Twelvers." Twelver Shiism was made the official religion of the Persian Safavid Empire in 1501, although the history of Shiism in Iran dates back to the seventh century. The Twelvers believe in twelve leaders, ordained by God, known as the Twelve Imams. They also believe the last Imam, Muhammad al-Mahdi, will one day return to the world as a messiah or *Mahdi*. The country is seen as a stronghold of the Shia Muslim faith; however, this has often led to clashes between the country's Shia majority and Sunni minority. Shia clergy have often dedicated themselves to missionary work among Sunnis to convert them to Shia Islam. This has led to high religious tensions, particularly during major Shia festivals. The country has also experienced ideological conflict with neighboring Arab countries due partly to the region's Shia-Sunni tensions, and partly due to ethnical tensions because Iranians are not ethnically Arab. Historically, Shias have been the victims of persecution across the Arab world, including in Iraq under Saddam Hussein and in Saudi Arabia; thus, Iranian national pride is very much intertwined with Shia religious pride.

Iraq

Iraq gained independence from Britain in stages. It was first declared an independent kingdom in October 1932 following Iraqi revolts over foreign rule, but the British still retained military bases in the region, as well as local militia and transit rights for their forces. The state later became a republic in July 1958 following a revolution against the British-installed monarchy. Iraq's religious demographics are officially 99 percent Muslim, with 60 to 65 percent practicing Shia Islam and 32 to 37 percent practicing Sunni Islam. The remaining population are 0.8 percent Christian and less than 1 percent Hindu. Iraq has been considered by many to be the birthplace of Shia Islam and contains many of its holy sites.

Iraqi nationalism stems from a historical identity that traces its origins back to ancient Mesopotamia and the civilizations of Babylonia and Assyria. Contemporary Iraqi national identity first came to prominence in the 1920s, at the same time as Arab nationalism, which largely explains its interconnected relationship. While technically separate, the two ideologies have greatly influenced each other. In the 1940s and 1950s, Iraq was at the forefront of the pan-Arabism movement, although fragmented national identity and regional attachments would lead to its decline. During his dictatorship, Saddam Hussein used both Iraqi nationalism and Arab nationalism to cement his political position and to legitimize his attempts to annex other territories in the Gulf. However, it is important to note there are native ethnic minorities within the region, such as the Chaldeans, who also can trace their heritage back to ancient civilizations but do not identify as Arab. The policy of Arab nationalism was seen as threatening to these populations.

Kuwait

The state of Kuwait was established in 1961. It became independent with the end of the British protectorate. The country has been largely characterized by its high levels of political freedom in comparison to other Gulf states. Prior to the 1990s, Kuwait and its neighbor to the north, Iraq, had a tense history, with Iraq's leaders claiming that Kuwait should be a territory of Iraq. However, relations improved during the Iran-Iraq War, which lasted from 1980 to 1988, when Kuwait provided assistance to Iraq. After the war's completion, Kuwait refused Iraq's request to forgive its $65 billion debt, and tensions mounted further when Kuwait began to increase its own oil production dramatically. The tipping point came in July 1990, when Iraq accused Kuwait of stealing Iraqi oil close to the Kuwait-Iraq border. One month later, Iraqi troops invaded and annexed Kuwait. After diplomatic solutions broke down, the United States led an international coalition to force Iraqi forces to withdraw. This conflict would later be known as the First Gulf War. When Iraqi troops did finally retreat, they carried out a scorched-earth policy of setting fire to Kuwaiti oil wells, thus doing irreparable damage to its economy. Largely due to its tense relationship with Iraq, nationalism in Kuwait is strong and reflects a strong sense of identity based on national affiliation; residents of Kuwait who may have Iraqi heritage, for example, can be denied Kuwaiti citizenship.

Members of the Kuwaiti volunteer army practice drills in the Saudi Arabian desert during the Gulf War.

Religious life in Kuwait is dominated by Sunni Muslims; however, the state does have a native Christian community. Kuwait is the only state in the Gulf Cooperation Council to allow citizenship rights to its Christian population.

Kuwait is often noted for its active public sphere, and its political and social organizations reflect a large degree of freedom. Unlike other Gulf states, Kuwaiti courts are secular, and sharia courts are not in use. The state consistently ranks as having the freest media in the Arab world. However, it is still only classed as "partly free" by the US political freedom and human rights organization Freedom House. During the 1960s and 1970s, Kuwait's press was believed to be one of the freest in the world, and many Arab writers moved to the country for increased freedom of expression, such as the Iraqi poet Ahmed Matar.

Oman

Unlike the majority of the Gulf states, Oman has a long history as an independent nation. It was not created out of foreign **colonialism** but traces its origins back to ancient times. As a result, it has a less strictly defined national culture and offers greater cultural diversity than many of its Arab neighbors. From 1507 to 1650, the country was held as a Portuguese colony, though the colony was attacked numerous times by Ottoman Turk invaders. By 1741, however, both the Portuguese and competing tribes had been pushed out of the region by an Omani tribe, which then established a line of sultans that continues to this day.

Oman's religious demography is similarly unique, with the majority of the population being Ibadi Muslims. The Ibadi movement is largely unknown, even to other Muslim denominations, but it is thought to predate both Sunni and Shia Islam. Though often described as puritanical, the Ibadi movement is both moderate and tolerant of other religions. Yet, the austere nature of Ibadism has greatly affected everyday life. Sharia (Islamic law) is strictly enforced in both public and private. Omani mosques are very simple and clean, with almost no decoration; they often even lack minarets.

The school of thought that Ibadism promotes, known as *Ibadhiyah*, is also dominant within Omani society. Ibadhiyah is opposed to armed rebellion and political assassinations and instead encourages harmony with other societies and, in particular, with other Muslim denominations. Founded in Basra in the seventh century, it is believed that the denomination was founded just twenty years after the death of the Prophet Muhammad. Today, Ibadi beliefs differ from other Muslim denominations in several ways:

- Unlike Sunnis, Ibadis do not believe that God will appear on the Day of Judgment;
- Also unlike Sunnis, Ibadis believe that the Quran (the religious book of Islam) was literally created by God, and not simply the word of God;
- They interpret the Quran's references to God as symbolic rather than literal;
- Ibadis believe all events are caused directly by God;
- In contrast to both Sunnis and Shiites, Ibadis believe a single leader for the Muslim world is unnecessary and that a community can rule itself if there is no fit candidate;
- They also disagree that a Muslim leader must be descended from the same tribe as the Prophet Muhammad, in contrast to Sunnis and Shiites;

The Sunni-Shia Divide

When the Prophet Muhammad died in 632 CE, disputes arose over the question of a successor. Some believed that the leader should be decided by consensus, while other believed only the descendants of the Prophet should be eligible. After some debate, the title of *caliph* (successor) was passed to Muhammad's trusted aide, Abu Bakr, and then to two successors who were both assassinated. This was done against the wishes of those who believed that Muhammad's son-in-law Ali was his designated successor. Eventually the title was given to Ali. After Ali's death, his sons Hasan and Hussein claimed the title. However, in 680 CE, Hussein and many of his relatives were massacred. Hussein's death made him a martyr in the eyes of Ali's followers, and this martyrdom became an important part of their faith. These followers became known as Shiites, from the phrase *shiat Ali*, or "followers of Ali."

The followers who believed in consensus and the legality of caliphs not descended from the Prophet became known as Sunnis. This was taken from the word *Sunnah*, or "prophet's tradition."

It is believed that because of the different paths the two sects took, Sunnis emphasize God's power in the material world, while Shiites revere martyrdom and sacrifice. Most Islamic societies have a Sunni majority and, in such societies, Shiites often make up the poorest section of society. Unfortunately, in many countries Shiites have had to hide their beliefs or suffer prejudice due to their denomination.

- Unlike Shiites, Ibadis do believe it is acceptable to conceal one's religious beliefs under certain circumstances;
- In terms of legal practice, absolute authority is given to the Quran, a practice in line with Shia beliefs but not Sunni beliefs.

Qatar

Qatar (pronounced like KAH-tr) gained independence from Britain in 1971. The state had previously been a British protectorate. Then, in 1968, Britain officially announced its intention to politically disengage from the Gulf region in three years. Initially, Qatar looked to join Bahrain and several other states in a federation. Regional disputes soon caused Qatar to resign and declare full independence instead. With the discovery of oil in the 1950s, the country's new wealth funded the expansion and modernization of Qatari infrastructure.

Islam, in the form of state-sponsored Wahhabism, permeates Qatari culture. Religious demographics for the country break down as 77.5 percent Muslim and 8.5 percent Christian. Qatar's Christian community is compromised largely of foreign expatriates, a mix of Europeans, North and South Americans, Asians, and Africans. The remaining 14 percent of the population is primarily Hindu, who are often members of the immigrant worker community. The Qatari constitution provides for freedom of religion, although there are certain restrictions placed on non-Muslim public worship.

City skyline in Doha, Qatar

After Saudi Arabia and Oman, Qatar is the most conservative society in the Gulf region. The use of sharia is a vital part of its legal system. Flogging is used as punishment for alcohol consumption, adultery, and premarital sex. Stoning is also a legal punishment, and homosexuality is punishable by death. Often, in family courts, a female's testimony is only worth half that of a man's, and in some cases, a female witness's testimony is not accepted at all. Journalists are subject to prosecution for criticizing or insulting Islam.

Saudi Arabia

The Kingdom of Saudi Arabia was established in September 1932. Its national culture is heavily influenced by both Arab civilization and Wahhabi Islam. It is often perceived as one of the most conservative states in the region.

Within the country, the state religion is Islam, and its law requires all citizens to be Muslims. There is no freedom of religion, even for foreigners. Islam is a major facet of Saudi identity, and the country is often perceived as the "cradle of Islam." This is largely because it is the site of two of the holiest cities of Islam: Mecca and Medina. Muslims are required to travel to Mecca for *hajj*, or a pilgrimage. Mecca is situated in the Hejaz region of Saudi Arabia and is the birthplace of the Prophet Muhammad, as well as the site of his first revelation of the Quran. It is both Islam's holiest city and also the direction of Muslim prayer. (Muslims must face the Kaaba, considered the "House of God," in Mecca every time they pray). For much of its history, Muhammad's descendants, called *sharif*, ruled over Mecca. Medina is also located within the Hejaz region and is known as the burial site of the Prophet Muhammad. It is Islam's second holiest city after Mecca. Medina was also the capital of the Muslim Empire under Muhammad and served as the power base of Islam during its early history. In both Mecca and Medina, non-Muslims are forbidden from entering the sacred center of the city. Linked with the birth of Islam, Saudi Arabia is

Pilgrims circumambulate the Kaaba in Mecca, Saudi Arabia.

also the birthplace of the Arabic language, which is the language of the Quran.

Ultraconservative Wahhabism, a branch of Sunni Islam, is a major feature of Saudi culture. Many of its followers find the terms "Wahhabi" or "Wahhabism" derogatory, and prefer to be known as "Salafi." Wahhabism was named after the eighteenth-century preacher and scholar Muhammad ibn Abd al-Wahhab. He lived in the region of Najd (now part of modern-day Saudi

Arabia) and founded a Muslim revivalist movement intended to remove "impurities" and "idolatry" from local Islamic practices: for example, the worship of local saints and the visitation of shrines and tombs. Later, he formed an alliance with local leader Muhammad bin Saud, founder of the House of Saud, offering political obedience in return for protection and aid in spreading Wahhabi **doctrine**. Through the Al Saud dynasty, the Wahhabi movement would gain access in the twentieth century to oil revenues. This enabled its supporters to further spread Wahhabi doctrines through investment in media, schools, universities, mosques, scholarships, and jobs for journalists, academics and Islamic scholars. In Saudi Arabia, Wahhabi scholars have gained prominent positions in education, law, and religious institutions and are able to heavily influence public policy in these areas.

The modern-day tenets of Wahhabism include the forbidding of all stimulants, including alcohol and tobacco, and the requiring of modest dress. For women, this means wearing an *abaya*, a long black garment that covers everything but the eyes and hands. What makes Wahhabism particularly unique is its strict avoidance of non-Islamic practices and non-Muslim friendship. (Atheism is also considered a capital offense.) This is largely due to a desire to avoid imitating non-Muslims' behavior. Senior leaders within Saudi Wahhabism have also promoted the idea that Islam forbids women to travel or work outside of the home without her husband's permission. Though women's rights have not often been prioritized in Saudi Arabia, recent years have seen some positive developments, such as the granting of female suffrage in December 2015. This has been largely due to the slow increase of local women's lobby groups, and the involvement of an increasing number of powerful Saudi businesswomen appealing to Saudi leaders who wish to portray a more progressive image to the West. Both Sunnis and Shiites have criticized Wahhabism for its fanatical practices, describing bin Saud's agreement to spread Wahhabism through militant jihad as more akin to traditional Najd practices of raiding than to the historical spread of Islam.

United Arab Emirates

The United Arab Emirates (UAE) was established in December 1971. It is a federation of seven emirates, or political territories: Abu Dhabi, Ajman, Dubai, Fujairah, Ras al-Khaimah, Sharjah, and Umm al-Quwain. It had previously been administrated and protected by the United Kingdom; however, by 1966, the British government could no longer afford to do this. In an attempt to protect themselves against outside political threats, the rulers of Abu Dhabi and Dubai formed a political union, created a constitution, and invited other emirates to join. Four other emirates agreed, though Bahrain and Qatar declined offers to join. In 1972, Ras al-Khaimah became the last emirate to join the UAE. This combination of numerous emirates has led to a diverse Emirati culture based on Arabian culture, but also heavily influenced by Iran, India, and East Africa.

The state religion is Islam, and the emirates hold a large Sunni majority at 85 percent with the remaining 15 percent practicing Shia Islam. Officially, the population is 76 percent Muslim and 9 percent Christian. The other 15 percent of the population

The UAE consists of seven different territories, all with their own cultures and dialects.

primarily consists of Hindus and Buddhists but also includes Baha'i, Druze, Ahmadi, Ismaili, Dawoodi Bohra Muslim, and Jewish citizens.

Islam holds a key place in public life, and Emirati law is structured around sharia. Flogging is used as punishment for capital offenses, such as adultery, premarital sex, and alcohol consumption. During the holy month of **Ramadan**, in which

Muslims are expected to fast between the hours of sunrise and sunrise, it is illegal to publicly eat, drink, or smoke. Blasphemy is also illegal. The UAE's application of sharia in criminal and family law has been heavily criticized by international observers due to its systematic discrimination against women.

Yemen

Like Oman, Yemen has an ancient history that is greatly influenced by Islam. Its culture, however, is distinctive from its neighbors, with more similarities to the Horn of Africa than to the rest of

Religious divides within Yemen have in recent years erupted into civil war.

Arabia and the Middle East. Prior to unification in May 1990, the country had been divided into North Yemen and South Yemen.

It is estimated that Yemen's population is 99.1 percent Muslim. Roughly 55 percent are Sunni Muslims and 45 percent are Shiites. The country's Sunni-Shia divide has led to tension in both political and civil life. In 2004, **dissident** Shia cleric Hussein Badreddin al-Houthi led an uprising against the Yemeni government. The reasoning behind the act was the need to protect the Shia community from government, and, implicitly, Sunni aggression. The Houthis, a Shia movement from northern Yemen, executed a successful takeover of the Sunni government in 2015, leading to the outbreak of an ongoing civil war.

The crossover of religion to Yemeni public life is an example of Islamist influence in the country. Islamism, or political Islam, is a movement characterized by moral conservatism and attempts to enforce Islamic values in all spheres of life. Islamists seek to reorder a particular country's government and society to align with sharia. While there are Islamist factions in many Arab states, they are more commonly found in countries where state failure has taken place.

Egyptian Muslims at prayer

3

Modern-Day Religion, Philosophy, and Nationalism in the Levant

The Levant region is a geographical term for a large area situated in the eastern Mediterranean. This area contains the states of Egypt, Jordan, Lebanon, Israel, Palestine, and Syria. In certain contexts, this can also include Turkey and Cyprus. Arabs comprise the largest cultural-linguistic group in the region, primarily due to the Arabization of the region from the seventh century onwards. Most populations speak Levantine Arabic, also known as Mediterranean Arabic, and even in Israel, where the primary language is Hebrew, Arabic is still an official language though a minority one in practice. The Levant is often described as the crossroads of western Asia, the eastern Mediterranean, and northeast Africa.

Muslims are the region's largest religious group, with the majority of these following Sunni, Wahhabi, or Shia Islam. However, there are still significant minorities in each country of Jews, Christians, Yazidi Kurds, Alawites, Nizari, Druze, and Ismailis. Prior to the 1948 creation of the state of Israel, Jews lived through the Levant alongside other religious groups, but since then almost all Jews have been exiled to Israel. Philosophy and cultural identity throughout the region is marked by contrasting beliefs and practices. Culturally ingrained values of hospitality, honor, and religious freedom find themselves sorely tested in states with high religious and tribal tensions. Religious discrimination continues to cause conflict, even as strides are taken to make societies more tolerant. Unsurprisingly, the family continues to hold a sacred place within the Levant, as it does in much of the rest of the Middle East, though definitions of what constitutes the family and what is owed to the family may vary.

Nationalism throughout the Levant has struggled with the need to balance the interests of individual countries with wider ideals of pan-Arabism. As we will see in this chapter, the Levant has historically differed from the Gulf by placing greater emphasis on state nationalism than ethnic nationalism.

Egypt

Egypt has a long cultural history; however, its arrival as an independent modern state began in February 1922 with its declaration of independence from Britain. The actual withdrawal of British military presence from the country took much longer—it lasted until 1954. The Egyptian Revolution of 1952 led directly to the overthrow of the British monarchy and the establishment of an Egyptian Republic. Since the rise of the Republic, Egyptian nationalism has emphasized the unity of Egyptians regardless of ethnicity or religion. Former president Gamel Abdel Nasser rose to power using themes that mixed Arab and Egyptian nationalism and framed Egypt as both a leader of Arab states and as a defender of Arab unity against the West and Israel. He helped to establish the short-lived United Arab Republic in 1958. However, his successors, including ousted leader Hosni Mubarak, quickly removed Arab nationalism from Egyptian identity and sought instead to re-emphasize Egyptian nationalism based on its distinctiveness from the rest of the Arab world. Since the Arab Spring in 2011, there have been international concerns on whether Egypt's secular nationalism can or will continue in its new political landscape.

Islam is the state religion and is practiced by around 90 percent of the population with the majority of its followers practicing Sunni Islam. Egypt has traditionally been a center of politics and culture for the Muslim world. In fact, its capital, Cairo, is famous for its Islamic architecture and has been christened "The City of 1,000 Minarets." Shiites make up a smaller population of Egyptians than Sunnis, however, and often face widespread discrimination.

The country is also home to Coptic Christians and other Christian denominations, which make up the remaining 10 percent of the population. The Copts are an ethnoreligious group predominant in North Africa and the Levant region. The Coptic Orthodox Church is the largest Christian Church in Egypt and Northeast Africa and belongs to the Oriental Orthodox family of churches. The church has a long history and, according to Coptic tradition, was founded by the apostle Saint Mark in the first century. During the regime of Gamel Abdel Nasser, Arab nationalist sentiment and policies negatively impacted Copts who identified strongly as non-Arab. During this time, church construction was purposefully delayed and many Christian religious courts were closed. Since 2011, discrimination of Egyptian Christians has increased, with attacks on churches and the kidnappings of Coptic Christian women and girls becoming increasingly common. Officially, Egypt only recognizes three religions: Islam, Christianity, and Judaism. Other faiths are not recognized by the Egyptian government and face persecution. They are often labeled as far-right groups that threaten national security.

Social structures are highly influenced by traditional Egyptian values of family, honor, and social class. The family is the bedrock of Egyptian society and kinship plays an important role in all social interactions. However, the individual is always subordinate to their family (including both the immediate nuclear family and the extended family), tribe, or social group. Nepotism, or the practice of those in power to offer jobs to friends and relatives, for instance, is regarded in a positive light as helping one's family. Similarly, honor plays a key role in interpersonal relationships, and is both a right and an obligation. An individual's honor or lack thereof affects the reputation of everyone in their family. It dictates that Egyptians must show hospitality to friends and guest, dress as well as they can afford, and defer to elders and authority figures. It also implies that a person's word is their bond, and to break one's word is to bring dishonor on one's entire family.

Israel

The modern creation of the state of Israel is very complex. Created in May 1948 when the British Mandate for Palestine ended, the state of Israel was an important refuge for Jews who had faced persecution in Europe during World War II. Israel was not recognized internationally until a year later, and there are still countries around the world that do not acknowledge Israel as its

The Temple Mount in Jerusalem continues to be a focal point for religious conflict and political negotiations.

own state. Israel's diverse culture reflects its diverse population; Jewish diasporic communities have settled in Israel from around the world, bringing their individual beliefs and traditions with them and adding to the national culture. Israel is the only country in the world where life is planned around the Hebrew calendar. The Zionist movement also largely shapes Israel's nationalist identity. Beginning in the late nineteenth century, this was a nationalist and political movement that supported the re-establishment of a Jewish homeland in the historic land of Israel. Integral to this movement was the revival of the spoken Hebrew language, which was previously spoken in the ancient Middle East. Since the establishment of the State of Israel, the movement has moved its focus to advocating internationally on behalf of Israel and tackling threats to its continued existence and security.

Another unique fact about Israel is that it is the world's only Jewish-majority state. Its Jewish population is made up of traditional, secular, and Haredi Jews, as well as Religious Zionists. Muslims are Israel's largest religious minority and the majority of Israeli Arabs are Sunni Muslims. Relations between religious groups, such as Jews and non-Jews, Muslims and Christians, and even different sects of Judaism, are often strained. Although Israeli law grants equal civil rights to all citizens regardless of religion, ethnicity, or heritage, the country was founded to provide a national home, safe from persecution, to the Jewish people. As such, the government does give preferential treatment to individuals who fall within the criteria of the Law of Return. This mandate, passed in 1950, allows foreign-born Jews and their families the right to live in Israel and to become Israeli citizens.

Religion is inseparable from the country's national identity and civil life. It has played a major role in Israel's history, largely due to its location on a major part of the Holy Land. This region is important to all Abrahamic religions (Judaism, Christianity, Islam, Druze, and the Baha'i Faith) because it is home to many sites that are pivotal in their religion's history. These sites include the Old City, the Temple Mount, the Western Wall, the Al-Aqsa Mosque, and the Church of the Holy Sepulchre. In Judaism, the Temple Mount is the most important religious site in the world. It is believed that the divine presence of God has manifested more times here than in any other place. Also, Jews believe that the world expanded out to its current form from this place, and that God created the first human using dust from the area. The Western Wall gains sacred status due to its proximity to the Temple Mount. Jewish and Christian prayer on the Temple Mount is forbidden, with only Muslims being allowed access. In Christianity, Jerusalem is revered for its role both in the Old Testament and in the life of Jesus. In Islam, Jerusalem is the third holiest city, after Mecca and Medina. Muslims believe that the Dome of the Rock stands over the Foundation Stone from which Muhammad ascended to Heaven.

Jordan

The Treaty of London granted Jordan independence from Britain in March 1946. Signed by both the British government and the Emir of Transjordan, Abdullah I, this treaty dictated the terms by which Jordan would become its own monarchy with Abdullah as

Women in Islam

It is a common stereotype in the West that Islam is inherently oppressive to women. Muslim women, like their Western counterparts, have had to struggle against gender inequality and discrimination, however such issues often are rooted more in diverse cultural traditions rather than religious ones.

Women's rights in Islamic societies continue to be a complicated and often oversimplified issue.

Islam, in fact, gave rights to Muslim women that were not available to Western women until the nineteenth century. For example, the Quran explicitly states that men and women are equal, gives women the right to own property and the right to divorce in certain cases, and requires the equal education of boys and girls. The key issue comes in how a given society chooses to interpret these rights. Most Middle Eastern countries allow women to vote, work outside the home, and run for office; however, custom is not always as liberal as the law allows. For example, in Saudi Arabia women can vote, work, and have excellent access to education, but they are legally required to wear a veil, are banned from driving, and are largely segregated from men. Yet, Islam is interpreted in many different ways in regard to its attitude towards women. Some Islamic scholars today advocate an Islamic feminism using the basic texts of Islam as justification.

its king. Jordanian nationalism believes all people of Jordan to be part of the Arab Nation, and this may account for the Jordanian people's open hospitality and tolerance toward other religions and ethnicities. In past years, the country has given asylum to Iraqi Christians fleeing persecution and has, to date, taken in over 1.4 million Syrian refugees. While the country is considered liberal in comparison to other Arab states, religion and tradition still play a major role in modern Jordanian society, and this balance has been severely tested by globalization.

Muslims make up 97 percent of Jordan's population, with the majority identifying as Sunni. Muslims wishing to convert to another religion face huge societal pressure and the loss of civil rights. The rest of the religious population is made up of Christians, Druze, and Baha'i. Relations between Muslims and Christians remain reasonably good; however, the smaller minorities such as the

Bedouin culture is largely nomadic and has influenced a number of cultures within the Levant.

Baha'i and Druze continue to face governmental discrimination. Jordan's constitution guarantees freedom of religion unless the practice of it violates public order or morality.

Many Jordanian traditions come directly from **Bedouin** culture, particularly hospitality customs and etiquette. The host must serve generous amounts of food and drink and ensure guests are comfortable and stay for as long as they like. A more specific example can be seen in the serving of coffee. The host must drink out of the cup first to check its temperature before it is passed to the guest. Displays such as these are known as *karam*, an Arabic word for "generosity" or "hospitality."

Lebanon

Lebanon, much like Egypt, had a lengthy journey to independence. It first declared independence in November 1943; however, the joint UN and French mandate did not end until October 1945. Later still was the withdrawal of French troops in December 1946. Lebanon sits at the crossroads of the Mediterranean Basin and the Arabian hinterland. This key location has greatly influenced its history and diverse cultural identity. Its society holds similarities to Mediterranean European culture; its population speaks Lebanese Arabic, which incorporates French and English words; and its artistic traditions combine both Mediterranean and Levantine norms. Writer Craig Davis has described Lebanon as a "rare environment that [is] at once Arab and European."

The country itself is the most religiously diverse in the Middle East, with several main religions and eighteen recognized religious sects. Its population includes both Shia and Sunni Muslims; Christian denominations including Maronites, Greek Orthodox, and Melkites; Druze; Jews; Baha'is; Hindus; and Mormons. Though Lebanon is a secular country, the religious authority of the individual's faith handles family affairs, such as marriage and inheritance. Religion in Lebanon is also unique in that it dictates the political makeup of the government. Under the terms of the National Pact, an agreement drawn up between the various political and religious leaders of Lebanon, the president must be a Maronite, the Prime Minister must be a Sunni, and the Speaker of Parliament must be a Shiite. Lebanon's demographics have shifted dramatically over the last century. At the beginning of the twentieth century, Lebanon was multisectarian with a majority Sunni Muslim and Christian population. Maronite Christians in particular held a significant influence over the government. However, members of Lebanon's significant Muslim population grew unhappy with the pro-Western attitudes displayed by their government prior to the Second World War. After the establishment of Israel, a huge influx of Palestinian refugees into the country led to a demographic shift and increasing tensions. This eventually led to civil war that lasted from 1975 to 1990.

Artistic freedom and freedom of the press are extremely important in Lebanese culture. At the beginning of the twentieth century, Lebanon's capital, Beirut, vied with Cairo as a cultural center for modern Arab thought and was home to many newspapers, magazines, and literary societies. After the country gained independence, Beirut became the epicenter of publishing within the Arab world and is characterized by a free and liberal media, as well as a progressive literary scene. According to Reporters Without Borders, the media have more freedom in Lebanon than in any other Arab country, though they still face political and judicial "machinations."

Palestine

As is well known, the national histories of Israel and Palestine are intertwined along lines of geography, religion, and ethnicity. In terms of its appearance as a modern-day state, the Palestine Liberation Organization (PLO) as a government in exile declared Palestinian independence in November 1988. Its nationhood claims include the territory of the West Bank and the Gaza Strip with East Jerusalem as its declared capital. Its establishment was triggered in part by the Palestinian exodus, also known as the *Nakba*, which means "disaster" or "catastrophe" in Arabic, when more than 700,000 Palestinians fled or were expelled from their land during the 1948 Palestinian war. Many of the affected and their descendants remain refugees today. Their right to return and their right to compensation are still major issues of the Israeli-Palestinian conflict. In 1993, the Palestinian Nation Authority was established following the transfer of increased control of Muslim holy sites in Jerusalem from Israel to the Palestinians. It was granted United Nations General Assembly (UNGA) observer state status in November 2012, which was a major step in symbolically recognizing Palestinian sovereignty. Unlike other Arab countries, Palestine has rejected pan-Arabism in favor of Palestinian self-determination due to its unique challenges. It

Palestinian citizens were forced to flee their homes after bomb attacks in Jerusalem in February 1948.

likewise rejects the historic occupation of the Palestinian territories by Israel. Many countries around the world still refuse to recognize Palestinian statehood, however, and conflicts break out often in the Israeli-occupied territories of the Gaza Strip, the West Bank, and the Golan Heights, where severe restrictions are placed on its inhabitants, thus limiting their civil rights.

The Israeli-Palestinian conflict has been one of the defining issues of the twentieth-first century. While there have been many attempts to form a peace treaty, issues such as political recognition, the drawing of borders, control of Jerusalem, and the Palestinian right of return continue to be fiercely debated. In 1993, Israeli officials and PLO leaders made significant progress by establishing a Palestinian agreement to Israel's right to exist. In 2000, Palestinian president Yasser Arafat and Israeli prime minister Ehud Barak met with US President Bill Clinton for the Camp David Summit. The offer made to Palestine was for a nonmilitarized state containing a large majority of the West Bank, with some parts of East Jerusalem and the entire Gaza Strip. However, it denied Palestinians the right to return to Israel and the control of religious sites, and also gave Israel control over the Jordan Valley. Arafat rejected this offer. Peace talks made more significant progress in 2001 at the Taba Summit in Egypt, but negotiators ran out of time before signing an agreement. In 2014, increased tension between Israel and Hamas, an Islamic fundamentalist organization that has governed the Gaza Strip since 2007, resulted in the Israel-Gaza conflict. This conflict lasted only seven weeks yet resulted in many Palestinian civilian deaths. A ceasefire deal was eventually brokered with the help of Egypt in November 2014.

Palestine's population is predominantly Muslim with the majority practicing Sunni Islam. Christianity still has a foothold in the region, though a minority one. The number of Palestinian Christians is estimated to be between 40,000 and 200,000, making up around 6 percent of the population.

Both religious freedom and discrimination shape public and private life in Palestine. While Palestine does not have a constitution, it does have the Basic Law. This law states that Islam is the official religion but also calls for tolerance and respect for other religions. Yet despite this, there are numerous incidents of abuse and discrimination between Christians and Muslims, and relations between Jews and non-Jews are often strained due to the ongoing Israeli-Palestinian conflict. A particular source of aggravation is Israel's control of access to sites holy to Christians and Muslims. Prevailing social attitudes are also a major barrier to interfaith marriage and conversion. Christians and Muslims are heavily encouraged to marry with their faith groups, and couples who challenge this norm face heavy familial and social opposition.

Syria

Syria achieved independence from the joint French and UN mandate on October 24, 1945. As well as a turbulent political history, Syria has a traditional society that places importance on family, religion, education, self-discipline, and respect. In the past, Syrian nationalism has often advocated for a "Greater Syria," based on ancient boundaries of the region that would stretch the country from southern Turkey through Lebanon and Palestine and into Jordan and Iraq.

Syria is a secular state with a range of faiths and sects. Around 74 percent of its population is composed of Sunni Muslims. Other religious minorities include Arab Alawites, Christians, Druze, and Shiites. However, Syria's Sunni population is not entirely Arab. Most of its Kurdish citizens are Sunni Muslims as well. What is notable about Syria's religious life is the geographic location of its religious minorities. Most Christians live in Damascus, Aleppo, Homs, and other large cities. Most Alawites lives in the country's coastal areas, and most Druze live in the Jabal al-Arab, a mountainous region in the southwest of the country. Syria's Shia citizens are concentrated in the rural areas of Homs. Religious divides have also greatly influenced the country's current civil war, with Alawite-dominated government troops fighting against Sunni-dominated rebel forces.

Despite, or maybe because of, its numerous faiths, Syrian people place a high value on traditional folk spiritual beliefs and practices. Many of the population believe strongly in the powers of good and evil, as well as in local saints. Many of these practices can be seen especially among Bedouin citizens who use amulets, charms, and incantations as protection against spirits and the evil eye. Among non-Bedouin populations, most villages have a local shrine where a particular saint is prayed to for aid, good fortune, or protection. In many cases, members of different faiths pray at the same shrine and people routinely worship saints who were members of other religious sects.

Casablanca in Morocco houses the third largest mosque in the world.

4

Modern-Day Religion, Philosophy, and Nationalism in North Africa

North Africa is, unsurprisingly, the northernmost area of the African continent. It consists of the Arab-African countries of Libya, Algeria, Morocco, and Tunisia. The United Nations also includes Sudan and the disputed territory of Western Sahara in its description of the region. The official language of most North African countries is Arabic, and its largest ethnic groups are Berbers, Arabs, and Africans.

Its people predominantly practice Islam, though there are also significant Jewish and Christian minorities.

Religion in North Africa takes elements from both its Arab conquerors and older native beliefs. Daily practice is often a blend of traditional Islam, with its rituals and principles, and earlier beliefs in spirits, the evil eye, special rites to gain good fortune, and the worship of local saints. The strong Islamic faith in these countries has led to the use of sharia, often based on Maliki doctrine. The Maliki school is one of the four major schools of religious law within Sunni Islam. It uses the Quran and sayings of the prophet Muhammad (also known as *hadiths*) to decide on the legality of issues and suitable punishments for crimes. If both of these sources are unclear, then the consensus of the population of Medina is taken as the deciding factor.

North African philosophy and cultural practices have a similarly dual heritage, depending which ethnicity the individual identifies with. Arabic-speaking northwestern Africans, regardless of background, often identify with Arab culture and identity. Yet this does not prevent them from also identifying with possible other heritages. Ethics throughout the region are diverse, but do share common ideas across ethnic groups. For example, in North African culture, many define ethics as a person's character. Thus, saying that someone has no morals would mean that they have no character. Character is decided by a person's deeds and conduct, meaning that it is not fixed and can change over time. At its most extreme, in some African cultures, to be a "person" is to be an adult human who exhibits moral virtues. Someone who behaves badly therefore is not a person, even if it is acknowledged that he or she is human. Unlike most Western beliefs, African ethics place more weight on the duties of the individual to behave in a prosocial manner rather than on rights per se.

As in other regions of the Middle East, nationalism within the countries of North Africa has its own overarching differences and sociopolitical agendas. The two competing ideologies within the region are pan-Arabism and Berberism. Pan-Arabism promotes the unification of all North African and West Asian countries from the Atlantic Ocean to the Arabian Sea. This effectively covers the entire area known as the "Arab world." It asserts that all Arabs are a single nation, often preaching socialist principles and strongly opposing Western political involvement in Arab affairs. It primarily seeks to empower Arab states from outside forces though the forming of alliances. The other dominant ideology of the region is Berberism, sometimes known as Amazighism. This is not just a political-cultural movement but also contains elements of ethnic and geographical nationalism. Berbers were the native population of North Africa prior to Islamic conquest, and many later adopted Islam and intermarried with Arab families. However, despite mixed Arab ancestry, this ethnic group still primarily identifies as Berber and holds to Berber language and customs. Those who identify as ethnic Berbers are often in opposition to the Islamist-driven cultural Arabization of pan-Arabism.

Algeria

Algeria is the largest country in the Arab world and gained independence from France in July 1962 following the Algerian

National Liberation Front soldiers captured by the Foreign Legion during the Algerian War of Independence

War of Independence. This conflict, known sometimes as the Algerian Revolution, was fought between French forces and the Algerian National Liberation Front (FLN) from 1954 to 1962. The war divided not only external and internal forces, but also the Algerian people themselves, with loyalists fighting for a French Algeria and nationalists striving for independence. When Algerian nationalist forces eventually won, more than 800,000 European-Algerians immigrated to France for safety. Loyalist forces were largely left alone as the peace treaty had ordered, but the volunteer Algerian auxiliaries (*Harki*) were labeled traitors, and huge numbers were murdered by the FLN or lynch mobs. The effect of the conflict shaped Algeria's political future for generations, leading directly to the election of nationalist leader Ahmed Ben Bella and to the widespread belief amongst the general population in the legitimacy of unrestricted force in pursuit of a worthy goal. Though the population is almost entirely ethnically Berber, only a small minority identify as Berbers. The majority of Algerians view themselves as Arabs first and foremost. Algeria is a recognized regional power within North Africa, as well as a founding member of the Maghreb Union. It has one of the largest militaries in Africa and imports most of its weapons from its ally, Russia.

Religious life in the country is dominated by the state religion of Islam with the majority practicing Sunni Islam of the Ibadi denomination. Ibadism is dominant in Oman and found in areas of North and West Africa. It is characterized by strict adherence to sharia and tolerant but somewhat puritanical practices. Islam is central to Algerian life as it is the basis upon which most citizens build their social and cultural identity and beliefs. Like some other countries, Islam is not just a religion but a way of life. Algeria's small Christian and Jewish minorities are estimated to stand at less than one percent of the population. Most practicing Christians are Pentecostal Protestants, and after the declaration of Algerian independence, most Jews migrated to France or Israel. Freedom of religion is included in the Algerian constitution, and the government does respect this, though with certain limitations. For example, while Algeria recognizes marriage between Muslim men and non-Muslim women, it does not recognize marriage between Muslim women and non-Muslim men. This is largely due to patriarchal lines of succession where men may pass down their cultural heritage to their children, but women cannot.

Philosophy within the country is largely divided along lines of gender, religion, and social ideology. This is seen most clearly in the competing ideologies of feminism and Islamism. During the 1962 War of Independence, women fought alongside men as equals, prompting a new sense of identity and a measure of acceptance from their male counterparts. Since this historic event, Algeria has been regarded as relatively liberal, and equality for women is enshrined in Algerian laws. Women can vote and run for political positions. Conversely, since the early 1990s, the country has also seen a sharp rise in Islamist sentiment, which has had a significant impact on Algerian society. In 1991, the Algerian authorities cancelled national elections due to fears over the popular election of an Islamist government. More women now wear the veil, some because they have become more conservatively religious, and some to avoid harassment on the street, on campuses, or at work. Islamist groups also prevented the enactment of more liberal family law despite pressure from feminist lobbies.

Libya

Libya gained independence from Italy in February 1947 and was later released from French and British oversight on December 24, 1951. The British and French governments held a joint mandate over Libya though the United Nations Trusteeship Council. The country has long considered itself part of the wider Arab community, and its culture is similar to its neighboring states. Its native population includes Arabs and Berbers, as well as other migrants of different nationalities. Libya's official language is Arabic, however, its spoken form is a colloquial dialect unique to the area around Libya. Under Colonel Muammar Qaddafi's

Tripoli in Libya under Italian conquest

dictatorship, teaching and speaking any foreign languages was banned. This included the native Berber language that thousands of Libyans nationals speak as their first language. Libyan heritage is intricately linked within the traditions of the nomadic Bedouin tribes. Most citizens use family names originating from Bedouin tribal ancestry.

The majority of Libya's population is composed of Sunni Muslims of either Ibadi, Sufi, or Ahmadi orders. Ultraconservative strains of Islam are becoming increasingly popular with the downfall of Colonel Qaddafi. There are also significant Christian and Jewish minorities. Most Christian communities within Libya are made up of foreign expatriates, and the largest denomination

Islamism vs. Fundamentalism

When describing Islamic political activities, the word "fundamentalism" is often used as a description. However, scholars have argued that using this term in fact shows a misunderstanding of the agendas involved. Fundamentalism concerns a desire to return to the original practice of a religion, yet for many modern Islamic political groups this is not correct. Islamism is a movement to create a new, modern, sociopolitical structure based on a strict reading of the Quran. Different Islamist groups have different aims: some want to create an Islamic state, while others want to make Islam the sole basis for law in society.

It is important to note that the vast majority of Muslims are not Islamists. They do not advocate violence nor do they necessarily want revolutionary religious-political change. However, some Muslims might agree with the anti-Western attitudes of the movement because they perceive the West to be spreading a corrupt value system, or because they resent Western involvement in national affairs. Others may simply desire to live in a society where Islam plays a greater role.

Islamism has traditionally been spread by wealthy Middle Eastern countries that could afford to provide financial resources to other countries with large Muslim populations. This financial aid has sometimes been used to affect the tone and practice of Islam within the receiving communities. For example, a country might give financial aid to another country on the condition that the community practices a more conservative version of Islam.

is Coptic Orthodox Christianity, known as the Christian Church of Egypt. There are also small numbers of Roman Catholics and Anglicans. Since proselytizing is illegal in Libya, people have been arrested on the suspicion of being Christian missionaries. In some parts of the country, Christians also face the threat of violence from radical Islamists. Before the Second World War, Libya had one of the oldest Jewish communities in the world; however, in 1942, the Italian Fascist authorities began setting up forced labor camps for Jews. Libyan Jews who were not interred in these camps were heavily restricted in their economic activity. Upon Libyan independence and the end of the war, most of the Jewish community emigrated.

One unique aspect of Libyan philosophy is the political-religious Sufi Senussi order. Sufism is a mystical denomination of Islam characterized by asceticism, which is the abstinence from worldly pleasures in order to gain closer communion with the divine. The Senussi are both a religious order and a tribe in Libya, but were first founded by the Grand Senussi Sayyid Muhammad ibn Ali as-Senussi in Mecca in 1837. The Senussi were primarily concerned with what they perceived as the decline of Islamic thought and the weakening of Muslim political integrity. Roughly one third of Libya's population strongly identifies with this movement. In the first half of the twentieth century, the Senussi fought both French expansion in the Sahara and the Italian colonization of Libya. National affiliation with the movement was galvanized in 1951 when the Grand Senussi's grandson became king, though he was later overthrown in the military coup that brought Colonel Qaddafi to power.

Morocco

Before becoming independent, Morocco was a protectorate of both France and Spain. The French protectorate ended in March 1956, and the Spanish protectorate followed a month later. Historically, Morocco has been home to many ethnicities, including Arabs, Africans, Berbers, and Jews. As a result, the country has managed to blend elements of Berber, Jewish, and Arabic heritage along with French, Spanish, and Anglo-American influences in order to create its own culture. Morocco has set the preservation of its cultural heritage amongst its top national priorities. The country's official languages are Berber and Arabic.

Islam dominates the religious atmosphere of Morocco. Most Moroccans practice Sunni Islam, but there are also Shia and Sufi orders. The King of Morocco himself stakes his legitimacy on being a descendant of the Muslim prophet Muhammad. The rest of the population is made up of Jews and Christians. Most Christians are either Roman Catholic or Protestant, and many are foreign residents. Native Christians often avoid meeting regularly due to fear of government surveillance and social persecution. There is also a very small minority who practice the Baha'i Faith. Though the Moroccan constitution does grant the freedom of worship and congregation to all, there are still limitations. Islam is the state religion and as such is granted rights by the constitution that vastly outweigh those given to other faiths. For example, since the law forbids the proselytizing of Muslims to any other belief, it is a criminal offense to possess a Christian bible written in the Arabic language.

The Hassan II Mosque in Casablanca, Morocco

Islam has also had great effect upon the creation of laws and social values in Morocco. One example is that of Mudawana, the personal status code or the family code of Moroccan law. This code relates to family issues such as marriage, divorce, polygamy, inheritance, and child custody. The code was designed on the principles of the Islamic Maliki school of Sunni jurisprudence and was later enshrined in the country's laws upon independence. Combined with modern progressive values, the code has greatly improved gender equality within Morocco. The code established joint responsibility for the family between men and women, limited the terms of polygamy and divorce, and granted women more rights to negotiate marriage contracts. Supporters of the reform have used the code as an example of how progressive reform can be framed within Islamic principles. Critics, however, have been quick to point out the elitist roots of the movement, the influence of Western principles, and the numerous barriers to implementation of the law within Moroccan society. In particular, these critics have pointed to the Moroccan judicial system's record of simply ignoring recently established laws, a lack of training among legal professionals in new laws, and ingrained practices of individual judges drawing on sharia instead of Mudawana. High levels of female illiteracy and strong traditionalist values combined with widespread poverty have further devalued these reforms, as well as a basic lack of awareness of the Mudawana's existence and provisions.

Tunisia

The Tunisian Republic gained independence from France in March 1956, and declared itself a republic just over a year later in July 1957. Culturally, the country has mixed influences from Phoenicians, Romans, Vandals, Byzantines, Arabs, Turks, Italians, Spaniards, and the French. Arabic is the official language, though its particular Tunisian colloquial form is known as Tounsi or Derja. French is also used commonly in education, the press, and for business purposes. It is the only democracy in the Arab world. Despite its

A Jewish synagogue in Tunisia

history as a secular state, since the Tunisian Revolution (which began in 2010 and led to the more widespread Arab Spring) this culture has come under threat from hardline Islamists promoting sharia as the main source for legislation.

Unlike in many Middle Eastern countries, in Tunisia, religion is kept separate from both political and public life. Tunisians are generally tolerant of religious freedom and tend not to inquire into others' personal beliefs. The population is predominantly Muslim, with the majority practicing Sunni Islam. In fact, the constitution states that Islam is the official state religion and requires the president to be Muslim. Despite this, Tunisians do enjoy a significant degree of religious freedom granted by the constitution, which guarantees freedom of thought, belief, and practice of religion. Roughly two percent of the population practices other faiths. Tunisia has a sizeable Christian community, with a majority of Catholics and some Protestants. The country's third-largest religion is Judaism. Most of Tunisia's Jewish population lives on the island of Djerba, home to the El Ghriba synagogue, which is one of the oldest synagogues in the world and considered by Jews to be a site of pilgrimage. The temple is believed to have been built using stones from Solomon's temple. Since the end of the Tunisian Revolution, also known as the Jasmine Revolution, in 2011, several Wahhabi sects have also emerged and, in some cases, have tried to violently repress any artistic expression that they perceive as hostile to Islam.

Artistic expression has been a major issue within Tunisia, both prior to the revolution and since. One effect of the revolution was that it changed the way in which art and politics interact within the country. Under the dictatorship of former president Zine al-Abidine Ben Ali, there were strict censorship laws governing freedom of expression. Since the revolution, artists have experienced unparalleled artistic freedom, but this has led to questions of how to use this new power. Similar problems have been seen in other countries affected by the Arab Spring. Pre-revolution, Tunisian artists were primarily concerned with finding ways around censorship. One particular method was known as collaborative painting. This is where several artists would work together on

a single piece of artwork without prior discussion or planning. Artists were perceived with such suspicion by the government that certain art schools were closed during the dictatorship as potential sources of rebellion. During the Revolution, artists began to use their increasing freedom to turn certain buildings and structures, previously symbols of the regime, into sources for new art. Examples include turning police stations into art galleries and burnt-out cars into sculptures. Villas owned by the Ben Ali family and their relatives became targets for graffiti artists. Since the end of the revolution, there has been a significant rise in street art in an attempt to reclaim public spaces once controlled by the government. Tunisian street art uses stencils, graffiti, and paintings to depict political or revolutionary themes, sometimes deploying Western and Latin American revolutionary icons. However, Wahhabi groups, and others following a strict interpretation of Islam, have vehemently condemned many modern artists and their works. Female artists in particular have come under threat by hardline Muslim groups. Similarly, the art community also faces challenges from the government. In November 2012, two graffiti artists were arrested for writing political slogans on the wall of a university. These included statements such as "the people want rights for the poor" and "the poor are the living-dead in Tunisia." They were charged with breaching the state of emergency, writing on public property, and disturbing public order.

Egyptian president Gamel Abdel Nasser

5

Important Figures in Religion, Philosophy, and Nationalism across the Middle East

The spread of different religions, philosophies, and forms of nationalism could not be accomplished, of course, without leaders to speak convincingly to the general population. Western audiences—and Middle Eastern audiences—might have different opinions regarding the important figures listed in this chapter; one person might be seen as a hero and a villain by different groups of people. However, each person listed below was influential in charting their country's path in political and/or religious aims.

The Gulf Region

Bahrain

Hamad ibn Isa Al Khalifah became Bahrain's first "king" in 2002; however, his family has ruled the country since 1783. The country has long been troubled by religious tensions, in particular having a majority Shia population ruled by a Sunni royal family. Between 2003 and 2010, both the king and his government came under fire by the Shia majority and were accused of corruption, discrimination in housing and jobs based on religion, and of bringing Sunni tribes into the country in order to change the nation's demographic composition. These tensions played out during the 2011 uprisings as part of the wider Arab Spring movement.

Iran

Reza Shah Pahlavi was Shah of Iran from December 1925 until he was forced to abdicate by Anglo-Soviet troops in September 1941. Pahlavi was a defining force in Iranian nationalism, though his insistence on forced detribalization resulted in the suppression of several ethnic and social groups. In an effort to destabilize the power of the clerical class and the nomadic tribes, he imposed changes in traditional attire, customs, and mores. He was responsible for changing the country's Western name from "Persia" to "Iran," a name that Iranians had historically used themselves. He frequently clashed with the clergy over his reforms and forbade photography that showed elements of Iran that he considered backwards, such as riding camels. Though the reasons for his Westernizing efforts have been debated and questioned by many modern historians, it

Iranian Shah Reza Pahlavi in 1930

is important to note that Reza's rise to power was helped in large part by the British government, which may explain his motivations.

Iraq

Nationalism played a key part in the political power of Saddam Hussein, the fifth president of Iraq. He first rose to prominence as a leading member of the revolutionary Arab Socialist Ba'ath Party, whose values were a mix of Arab nationalism and socialism. He played a key role in the political coup, also known the July 17 Revolution, that brought the party to power. Hussein's power relied heavily on the use of a cult of personality spread throughout Iraqi society that combined religious and nationalistic elements. In thousands of pictures displayed across the country, he was portrayed in different styles and costumes in appeal to different sections of society, including Bedouin costumes, traditional Iraqi peasant clothes, Kurdish dress, modern Western suits, and the full robe of a devout Muslim. In the Western media, he became notorious as the key threat to stability in the region, especially following his aggression in Kuwait. In 2003, the United States led an invasion of Iraq on the pretext of the country possessing weapons of mass destruction (which were later found not to exist). Hussein was eventually captured by US forces and charged by the Iraqi Special Tribunal. He was found guilty of crimes against humanity for his genocide against Iraqi Shiites in the 1980s and sentenced to death. He was hanged on December 30, 2006.

Kuwait

Sheikh Abd Allah al-Salim al-Ṣabaḥ was Kuwait's eleventh ruler, but its first Emir after the end of the British protectorate. Unlike his predecessors, his political views were more pro-Arab than pro-British, and Kuwaitis regard him as the founder of modern Kuwait. The 1950s and 1960s saw a wave of Arab nationalism across the Middle East. This, combined with the rise of Kuwait's intelligentsia and political revolutions in surrounding countries, helped to push change through. After ending Kuwait's protectorate status, Abdullah introduced Kuwait's constitution in 1962 and established the country's parliament in 1963. He died on November 24, 1965.

Oman

One of the most important figures in Oman is Ahmed bin Hamad al-Khalili, officially known as the Grand Mufti of the Sultanate of Oman. A Grand Mufti is the highest official of religious law in a Sunni Muslim country. He gives legal opinions or edicts, helps to interpret the Quran for legal affairs, and can issue a *fatwa*, or a ruling on a point of Islamic law. Ahmed bin Hamad al-Khalili regularly appears on national television to answer the nation's questions on Islam, and his opinions are extremely influential. During the uprisings known as the Arab Spring, he declared that gyms and health clubs were "dens of vice" and has previously tried to convince the government to ban alcohol.

Qatari royalty and women's rights advocate, Her Highness Sheikha Moza bint Nasser Al Missned

Qatar

Women's rights have become an increasingly important issue within Qatar, and one of its most well-known advocates is Her Highness Sheikha Mouza bint Nasser Al Missned. The second wife of the former Emir of Qatar, she has been a vocal advocate for women's issues, women's conferences, higher education opportunities, and the creation of a cabinet-level position in the government dedicated to women's concerns. When Sheikha bint Ahmed Al-Mahmoud became Qatar's first female cabinet minister and was appointed minister for education, she thanked Sheikha Mouza in particular for her support of women's rights. Qatari policies on gender equality are heavily influenced by Wahhabi interpretations of Islam, which are highly discriminatory toward women.

Saudi Arabia

One of the most important socioreligious bodies in Saudi Arabia is the Committee for the Promotion of Virtue and the Prevention of Vice. In January 2012, Abdul Latin Abdul Aziz al-Sheikh was appointed as its head. The committee is responsible for ensuring that Saudis and foreign residents respect traditional Islamic morality, as defined by the Saudi government. Upon his appointment, al-Sheikh identified five key areas of concern for his religious police force: preserving Islam, preventing blackmail, combating sorcery, fighting human trafficking, and ensuring obedience to the Saudi authorities. In the early days of the Arab Spring, he publicly decried the use of social media, claiming that anyone using sites such as Twitter "has lost this world and his afterlife."

Leaders on Film: Gamal Abdel Nasser

Former Egyptian President Gamal Abdel Nasser's iconic status has been enshrined in a number of films by Egyptian directors.

In 1963, the director Youssef Chahine produced *El Nasser Salah El Dine*, translated as *Saladin the Victorious*. The film intentionally drew parallels between the Arabic hero Saladin, who fought European forces for control of the Holy Lands, and Nasser and his pan-Arabist policies. The movie is commonly perceived to promote the ideal of pan-Arab unity through its depiction of various Arab nations fighting against European colonial powers.

In 1996, Mohammed Fadel directed *Nasser 56*. The film was set during the 1956 Suez Crisis and set a new record at the Egyptian box office. It quickly became a classic and gained huge popular appeal with Egypt's youth. It is now consider a milestone in Egyptian and Arab cinema as the first film to dramatize the life of a modern-day Arab leader.

United Arab Emirates

The creation of the UAE was driven largely by two key figures: the ruler of Abu Dhabi, Sheikh Zayid ibn Sultan Al Nahyan, and the ruler of Dubai, Sheikh Rashid ibn Said Al Maktum. On February 18, 1968, the two leaders shook hands at a meeting on the desert border between Dubai and Abu Dhabi and agreed to found a federation. This would later become the United Arab Emirates along with several other small kingdoms. Al Nahyan in particular was an advocate for cooperation and dialogue within the Middle East as a means to settle territorial disputes. Rashid ibn Said Al Maktum passed away on October 7, 1990. Zayid ibn Sultan Al Nahyan followed on November 2, 2004.

Yemen

Badreddin al-Houthi, a cleric and head of the religious Zaidi Shia sect, was an incredibly influential—and divisive—leader in Yemen. As the founder of the Houthi movement, al-Houthi claimed that the group's military actions were intended to fight against the expansion of Wahhabism in Yemen, while the government has accused it of intending to overthrow the regime and institute sharia. The Houthis have also been accused of receiving financial backing from the Shia Iranian government. Al-Houthi was killed during military action in 2004, but the Houthis have remained an important force in Yemen. Continuing tensions between Shia and Sunni sects within the country led to a Houthi government takeover in 2004 and, in retaliation, Saudi Arabian military operations.

The Levant Region

Egypt

One of the most iconic figures of the modern Middle East was the Egyptian president Gamal Abdel Nasser, who served from 1956 until his death in 1970. His rise to power was a precursor to a wave of political revolutions across the region. He is known for fighting the British and the French during the Suez Crisis of 1956, modernizing Egypt, and uniting the Arab world under pan-Arabist policies. His policies included social justice, Arab unity, modernization, and anti-imperialism. Yet, on the other hand, his critics have also accused him of authoritarianism and failure to establish civil institutions, and also suggested that his legacy set the template for dictatorial rule in Egypt for future generations.

Israel

David Ben-Gurion was the primary founder of the State of Israel and its first prime minister. For much of his life, Ben-Gurion was a major leader within the Zionist movement and was even appointed as Executive Head of the World Zionist Organization in 1946. He was the first person to sign the Israeli Declaration of Independence, which he also helped to write. In addition, he led the country during the 1948 Arab-Israeli War and united the various Jewish militias into the Israel Defense Forces (IDF). As a consequence of these actions, he is known as Israel's founding father. Critics of Ben-Gurion state that he set the tone for anti-Arab sentiment among some levels of Israeli society.

Polish-born Israeli statesman David Ben-Gurion

Jordan

The country's current king, Abdullah II, has ruled since February 1999. His family has ruled Jordan since 1921 and claim to be descended from the Prophet Muhammad. In November 2002, King Abdullah introduced the nationalistic slogan "Jordan First" to promote the concept of a modern democratic state. Its nationalist aim is to "consolidate the spirit of belonging among citizens, all acting as partners in building and developing Jordan." This slogan is reflective of King Abdullah's strides to encourage a Jordanian identity that encompasses all sections of its society. Other examples include his 2010 proposal at the United Nations to promote peace, his work to eliminate intolerance and discrimination based on religion or belief, and his focus on interreligious dialogue.

Lebanon

In the history of Lebanese independence, three figures are perceived as the founders of modern Lebanon. These are Bechara El Khoury, the first president of Lebanon; Riad al-Sulh, the first prime minister of Lebanon; and Emir Majid Arslan II, the first Lebanese minister of defense. All three men are widely regarded as national heroes for their part in Lebanese independence from the French. After the French arrested key members of the newly formed government, Christian and Muslim opinion quickly united, and massive street protests began. This led to international pressure demanding the release of the Lebanese leaders, including El Khoury, al-Sulh, and Arslan. The three men were also instrumental in creating the

National Pact, an agreement between Lebanon's religious leaders, which later formed the basis for the country's constitution.

Palestine

Yasser Arafat was Chairman of the Palestine Liberation Organization (PLO), President of the Palestinian National Authority (PNA), and leader of the Fatah political party and former paramilitary group. He spent most of his life involved in the oncoming territorial conflict between Israel and Palestine. However, Arafat is best known for his part in a series of negotiations with Israel to end the conflict between the government of Israel and the PLO. He later won a Nobel Peace Prize in 1994. The majority of Palestinians view him as a freedom fighter who symbolized the national aspirations of his people, while many Israelis regard him as an unrepentant terrorist.

Syria

One of Syria's biggest nationalistic debates has historically been over its borders. Antoun Saadeh, founder of the Syrian Social Nationalist Party (SSNP), is one of Syria's most famous nationalists. He advocated for a Syrian nation state called the "United Syrian Nation" or "Natural Syria" that included Lebanon, Iraq, Kuwait, Jordan, Palestine, Cyprus, Sinai, southeastern Turkey, and southwestern Iran as one single nation. His theory was based on geographical boundaries within the area and the common history of its people. He rejected Arab nationalism and advocated for a totalitarian system of government.

North Africa

Algeria

Ahmed Ben Bella was leader of the Front de Libération Nationale (FLN) and the first president of Algeria after gaining independence. The FLN is a socialist political party that led the main nationalist movement during the Algerian War. Ahmed Ben Bella was greatly influenced by Egypt's Gamal Abdel Nasser and his promotion of Arab nationalism. He firmly believed that militant Islamic groups had developed from an incorrect interpretation of Islam. Despite other controversies within his regime, he was well regarded for his role in the anti-colonial movement and is often perceived by Arab intellectuals as one of the last original Arab nationalists. Ben Bella passed away in 2012 at the age of ninety-five.

Libya

Muammar Qaddafi, widely known as "Colonel Qaddafi," was a Libyan revolutionary, politician, political theorist, and, later, dictator. He began his career in the military before founding a revolutionary cell within the military and seizing power in 1969 from the reigning monarch in a bloodless coup. Initially, Qaddafi promoted an agenda of Arab nationalism and socialism, but later came to shift his alliances to the pan-African movement. His supporters lauded him as a defender against imperialism and a promoter of African and Arab alliances. However, critics have condemned his rule as a dictator, highlighted the human rights abuses carried out under his regime, and linked him to the proliferation of tribal warfare and terrorism (including the bombing

King Mohammed VI of Morocco

of Pan Am Flight 103 above Lockerbie, Scotland, in 1988). In 2011, he was captured and killed by militant rebels during the Libyan Civil War.

Morocco

King Mohammed VI is the reigning monarch of Morocco. He came to the throne in 1999 upon the death of his father. From the moment of his ascension, Islamist conservatives fiercely opposed his reformist rhetoric. His reforms would later go on to anger many Muslim fundamentalists. In February 2004, he enacted the latest revision to the Mudawana, or "family code." This, among other things, granted women more legal power in family matters and was praised by progressive sections of Moroccan society. However, the King's reputation has also been marred by allegations of corruption as revealed in 2010 by leaked confidential documents.

Tunisia

Habib Bourguiba was a key figure in Tunisia's fight for independence against the French. He cofounded the political party Neo Destour, which spearheaded the country's independence movement. Upon independence, he became the country's first prime minster and later its first president in 1957. His presidency helped to create the modern Tunisian state, though his rule was authoritarian. He was finally overthrown by his prime minister Zine al-Abidine Ben Ali in 1987, who was overthrown himself in 2011 during the Arab Spring uprisings.

Habib Bourguiba spearheaded the campaign for Tunisian independence.

Chronology

570–632	Lifetime of Muhammad, Prophet of Islam.
632–661	The Rashidun Caliphate conquers and bring Islam to Persia, Egypt, and Iraq.
1774	Ottoman power over the Middle East begins to wane as its territories are taken over by European powers.
1902–1932	Wahhabi leader Abd al-Aziz ibn Saud captures the city of Riyadh and begins a thirty-year campaign to unite the Arabian Peninsula and create the Kingdom of Saudi Arabia.
1914–1918	World War I sees Arab states not under Ottoman rule join the British on the promise of independence after the war.
1916	British and French governments sign a secret deal to divide up land previously controlled by the Ottoman Empire into French- and British-administrated areas.
1917	The British sign the Balfour Declaration promising their support to establish a "National Home for the Jewish people" in Palestine.

1918–1922	Nationalist movement in Egypt leads to Egyptian independence.
1921	Reza Shah takes control of Iran.
1928	The Muslim Brotherhood is founded as an Islamic revivalist movement in Egypt.
1948	Jews return to their ancient biblical homeland, and the state of Israel is created.
1956	Egypt nationalizes the Suez Canal.
1979	The Iranian Revolution leads to the establishment of an Islamic Republic in Iran.
1980–1988	The Iran-Iraq War rages.
1990	The Gulf War begins when Iraq invades Kuwait.
2003	The US-led invasion of Iraq begins; Saddam Hussein goes into hiding.
2011	The Arab Spring spreads across the Middle East.
2014	The Islamic Caliphate is established by the self-claimed Islamic State (ISIS) in areas of Syria and Iraq and gains global support from radical Sunni Muslims.

Map of the Region

RUSSIA
KAZAKHSTAN
TAJIKISTAN
Caspian Sea
Black Sea
GEORGIA
Baku
TURKMENISTAN
Ashgabat
ARMENIA
AZERBAIJAN
Ankara
TURKEY
Kabul
Mashhad
AFGHANISTAN
Indus
Tehran
Kandahar
Tigris
SYRIA
IRAQ
Eşfahān
IRAN
Beirut
Damascus
Baghdad
LEBANON
ISRAEL
Amman
Jerusalem
JORDAN
Euphrates
Kuwait
KUWAIT
Persian Gulf
BAHRAIN
Manama
Abu Dhabi
OMAN
Tropic of Cancer
Muscat
Doha
Nile
Riyadh
QATAR
UNITED ARAB EMIRATES
Medina
OMAN
Aswān
SAUDI ARABIA
Arabian Sea
Red Sea
Mecca
Port Sudan
Nile
ERITREA
YEMEN
Asmara
Sanaa
Blue Nile
Aden
Gulf of Aden
Socotra
(YEMEN)
Lake Tana
DJIBOUTI
Djibouti
Hargeysa
White Nile
Addis Ababa
ETHIOPIA
SOMALIA
Indian Ocean
Juba
Lake Turkana
UGANDA
Mogadishu
Equator
KENYA
Kampala

Glossary

Arab Spring Democratic uprisings that swept through the Arab world in 2011, leading to the collapse of many governments and to civil wars, including in Libya and Syria; began in 2010 with the self-immolation of Tunisian street vendor Mohamed Bouazizi.

authoritarian A leader or regime that demands total obedience and refuses others' freedom to act as they wish.

Baha'i Faith A monotheistic religion that emphasizes the spiritual unity of all humankind.

Bedouin A nomadic Arab from the desert.

colonialism The practice of one country controlling another.

denomination A religious group with different beliefs or practices than other groups within the same religion.

dissident A person who publicly criticizes their government.

doctrine A set of beliefs that are taught by a particular group or religion.

Druze An Arabic-speaking ethno-religious group from Southwestern Asia.

Eurocentric The practice of viewing the world from a European perspective and the implied belief of European superiority.

imperialism A system where one country rules other countries, usually by force.

jurisprudence The study of law and the principles of law.

mandate Authority given to an elected group to perform an action or govern a country.

mullahs An educated Muslim trained in religious law and usually holding an official post.

protectorate A country that is controlled and defended by a more powerful country.

Ramadan The ninth month of the Muslim year, during which time Muslims fast during the day in order to commemorate the first revelation of the Qur'an to Muhammad.

secular Something that is non-religious.

shah Historical title given to emperors and lords of Iran.

sultan Historical Arabic title given to kings and emperors.

trade embargo The prohibition of commerce and trade with a particular country.

tribalism The state of being organized according to different tribes or tribal affiliations.

Yazidism An ethnically Kurdish religious community from northern Mesopotamia.

Zoroastrianism One of the world's oldest religions attributed to the teaching of the Iranian Prophet Zoroaster in approximately 1500 BCE.

Further Information

Books

Bonine, Michael, Abbas Amanat, and Michael Gasper, eds. *Is There A Middle East?:The Evolution of a Geopolitical Concept*. Stanford, CA: Stanford University Press, 2011.

Edwards, Brian T. *After the American Century: The End of U.S. Culture in the Middle East*. New York: Columbia University Press, 2015.

Lee, Robert D. *Religion and Politics in the Middle East: Identity, Ideology, Institutions, and Attitudes*. Boulder, Colorado: Westview Press, 2013.

Lewis, Bernard. *Faith and Power: Religion and Politics in the Middle East*. New York: Oxford University Press, 2010.

Sorenson, David S. *An Introduction to the Modern Middle East: History, Religion, Political Economy, Politics*. Boulder, Colorado: Westview Press, 2013.

Websites

CIA World Factbook: The Middle East

https://www.cia.gov/library/publications/resources/the-world-factbook/wfbExt/region_mde.html

This Central Intelligence Agency (CIA) resource is filled with key facts on all countries across the Middle East, ranging from society, geography, and transportation to military, security and transnational issues.

Islam in Oman

http://islam-in-oman.com/en/ibadhiyah.html

This government website was set up by Oman's Ministry of Endowments and Religious Affairs to promote interfaith dialogue and teach more understanding of Ibadhiyah Islam, and includes a video documentary.

PBS's Global Connections: The Middle East

http://www.pbs.org/wgbh/globalconnections/mideast/index.html

Public Broadcasting Station's educational resource on Middle Eastern culture, politics, and history features a wide range of information on religion, foreign relations with the United States, and a variety of issues.

Bibliography

Adelson, Roger. *London and the Invention of the Middle East: Money, Power, and War, 1902-1922*. New Haven, CT: Yale University Press, 1995.

Ahmed, Leila. *Women and Gender in Islam: Historical Roots of a Modern Debate*. New Haven, CT: Yale University Press, 1992.

Anderson, Ewan. *The Middle East: Geography and Geopolitics*. London, UK: Routledge, 2000.

Barzilai, Gad. *Wars, Internal Conflicts and Political Order*. Albany: State University of New York Press, 1996.

Bowker, Robert. *Egypt and the Politics of Change in the Arab Middle East*. Cheltenham, UK: Edward Elgar Publishing, 2010

Friedman, Saul S. *A History of the Middle East*. London, UK: McFarland & Company, 2006.

Friedmann, Yohanan. *Tolerance and Coercion in Islam: Interfaith Relations in the Muslim Tradition*. Cambridge, UK: Cambridge University Press, 2003.

Halliday, Fred. *Nation and Religion*. London, UK: Saqi Books, 2013.

Humphreys, R. Stephen. *Between Memory and Desire: The Middle East in a Troubled Age*. Berkeley, CA: University of California Press, 2005.

Joseph, Suad, and Afsaneh Najmabadi. *Encyclopaedia of Women & Islamic Cultures*. Boston: Brill, 2005.

Karsh, Efraim. *Islamic Imperialism: A History*. New Haven, CT: Yale University Press, 2006.

Lewis, Bernard. *What Went Wrong?: Western Impact and Middle Eastern Response*. Oxford, UK: Oxford University Press, 2002.

Mansel, Philip. *Levant: Splendour and Catastrophe on the Mediterranean*. New Haven, CT: Yale University Press, 2011.

Mansfield, Peter. *A History of the Middle East: 4th Edition*. London, UK: Penguin Books, 2010.

Noueihed, Lin, and Alex Warren. *The Battle for the Arab Spring: Revolution, Counter-Revolution and the Making of a New Era*. New Haven, CT: Yale University Press, 2012.

Potter, Lawrence G., ed. *Sectarian Politics in the Persian Gulf*. Oxford, UK: Oxford University Press, 2014.

Waines, David. *An Introduction to Islam*. Cambridge, UK: Cambridge University Press, 2003.

Index

Page numbers in **boldface** are illustrations. Entries in **boldface** are glossary terms.

About the Author

Katie Griffiths has written numerous several non-fiction books for middle- and high-school students on history, culture and mythology. For more information, visit www.katiegriffiths.org.